MW01109985

The Eastside Extra

WHY IS OUR LAKE OFF-LIMITS?

Inside Eastside's Polluted History

EPA SUPERFUND SITE

Written by Anita Storey • Illustrated by Nathalie Ortega

Book design by Sarah Taplin
Illustrations by Nathalie Ortega

Published in the United States by Jolly Fish Press, an imprint of North Star Editions, Inc.

This is a work of fiction. Names, characters, places, and incidents are either the product of the author's imagination or are used fictitiously, and any resemblance to actual persons living or dead, business establishments, events, or locales is entirely coincidental.

Library of Congress Cataloging-in-Publication Data (pending)
978-1-63163-655-4 (paperback)
978-1-63163-654-7 (hardcover)

Jolly Fish Press
North Star Editions, Inc.
2297 Waters Drive
Mendota Heights, MN 55120
www.jollyfishpress.com

Printed in the United States of America

WHY IS OUR LAKE OFF-LIMITS?

OFF-LIMITS?

Inside Eastside's Polluted History

Written by Anita Storey • Illustrated by Nathalie Ortega

Text by Maya Chhabra

JOLLY
FiSH
PRESS

Mendota Heights, Minnesota

CHAPTER ONE

A Neighborhood Puzzle

Benny, his little sister Isabel, and their parents all crammed into the crowded waiting area at the airport. People were holding up signs with the names of passengers on them, making it hard for Benny to see the passengers themselves. The travelers had just gotten off the plane and were coming through the glass doors in a steady stream. But despite standing on his tiptoes, Benny couldn't see his uncle anywhere.

"Bet you I spot Tío Jorge first," Isabel said.

Benny already had his eyes peeled, but now it

was a contest. He hadn't seen his father's brother in years and had only a hazy memory of what he looked like. Tío Jorge was a short, brown-haired man, but that description fit so many of the passengers! How embarrassing would it be if Isabel, who'd been so young last time their uncle visited, recognized him before Benny did?

Benny racked his memory for details. Tío Jorge sometimes wore a sports T-shirt, but Benny couldn't even remember what team it was, or what sport. Suddenly, he spotted a familiar-looking lime-green suitcase. The super-bright color was impossible to forget. It was worn out after all these years, and one wheel stuck and squeaked, slowing down the man rolling it. But it was still the same bag.

"There he is!" Benny nudged Isabel. "He's finally here. Tío Jorge!"

The man with the green suitcase grinned and started waving as he came toward them.

"I didn't think you'd recognize me," Tío Jorge said as he gave Benny a hug. "It's been too long, Benicio!"

"Please, call me Benny," he corrected his uncle, hoping Tío Jorge wouldn't realize that he had really recognized the luggage. "It's so great that you're here."

Isabel jumped up and down excitedly. "We're going to have so much fun!"

Tío Jorge laughed. "It's going to be the best vacation I've had in a long time. And I've got gifts for both of you in this bag." He patted the lime-green suitcase. "You can open them when we get home."

The ride home seemed to take forever. It wasn't that long of a drive, but Isabel talked nonstop the whole way. She kept trying to guess what her gift was, but Tío Jorge wouldn't tell her. He just laughed and said, "You'll have to wait!"

Back at the house, Benny and Isabel crowded around as their uncle opened his luggage.

Tío Jorge pulled out a long, wrapped present. It was too skinny to be a baseball bat, but Benny couldn't figure out what else could be that long.

"Can you guess what I got you?" Tío Jorge asked. He passed the present to Benny, who tore off the wrapping paper to reveal a long pole.

"A fishing rod?" Benny couldn't help frowning. He couldn't remember the last time he'd gone fishing.

"I fish all the time with my friends in their motorboat back home in Hialeah. And now I can go fishing with my nephew! I saw on the map that there's a lake just outside West Grove."

Benny knew he should be happy his uncle had brought him a present, but his heart sank. "No one ever goes fishing in that lake, Tío Jorge. Mom said it's off-limits."

Tío Jorge's jaw dropped. "You're kidding!"

"Nope. We're not allowed to swim in it either."

Disappointed, Tío Jorge cleared the wrapping paper from the floor and threw it in the trash. "Sorry, Benny. I should have checked. But that's really strange—why would a lake be off-limits?"

Benny shrugged. "I think Mom said something

about the water being bad." He'd never really thought about it. It was just one of the rules of West Grove, like no biking on the sidewalk. He and his friends went swimming at the public pool instead, so it wasn't a big deal.

But as Isabel opened her present—a boxed set of art supplies and glitter—Benny began to wonder about the forbidden lake. He pulled out his phone to text his best friends, Anika and Libby. This could be a story for their newsletter, *The Eastside Extra*.

———————

The three friends agreed to meet at the park. Libby and Anika got there first. Benny's message had talked about a "giant neighborhood puzzle," but he hadn't said what that puzzle was. Libby was relieved that their newsletter would have something to publish. It had been a slow summer. Not much had happened in their neighborhood of Eastside for almost a month.

Anika, who loved detective novels and dreamed of becoming a journalist, was anxious to find out what Benny's text meant. She kept trying to guess what the puzzle was.

"It could be anything!" she complained. "Is there hidden treasure? An unsolved mystery? I heard a bunch of bricks from the town hall fell down in the last thunderstorm. They could have hit someone."

"Wow, I hadn't heard about that," Libby said. "But I bet it's something much smaller. Life is full of little mysteries. Like why are my brothers obsessed with baseball? Why is my neighbor Mr. Grayson so mean? Why do my brothers play baseball near his fence when they know he hates kids and they could end up smashing his window by accident—which, by the way, they did?" Libby sighed. It had been a long day already, with her parents having to go over to personally apologize to their grumpy next-door neighbor.

"Are you sure it was an accident?" Anika asked, her investigative spark flaring. "They had a motive, because he's always been so rude to them."

Libby laughed. "Don't go all Sherlock Holmes on them!"

"Wrongdoers flee in terror before the private eye

of Eastside." Anika pretended to squint through a magnifying glass.

"Your magnifying glass can't see behind you," said a familiar voice.

Anika jumped, her thick ponytail swinging as she turned around quickly. "Benny, you scared me! What are you doing sneaking up on me like that?"

"And why are you holding a fishing pole?" Libby added.

"The pole is a piece of the puzzle," Benny said mysteriously.

"Come on, tell us," Anika begged.

"Tío Jorge likes to fish, so he brought me a fishing rod because he heard there was a lake in West Grove."

"Fishing isn't allowed," Anika pointed out. "Kind of a bad present."

"Yeah, but my uncle wouldn't know that. He doesn't live here, so he's never actually seen the lake."

"I don't think I've ever seen the lake either," Libby said, pausing to think for a moment. "Wait—is the lake the mystery?"

"Exactly." Benny waved the fishing pole for emphasis, nearly smacking Anika.

"Sorry! Sorry!" he said when she glared at him.

"Put that thing down before you hurt someone," Anika said. But she didn't stay mad long—she was too curious. "What do you think could have happened to the lake?"

"Whatever it was, it must have been really bad if we can't swim in it, fish in it, or even go near it," Libby said. "But I bet we could drive by and take pictures."

"That's a great idea! I'll ask my mom to take us there tomorrow." Benny was already thinking about what a great topic this would make for their newsletter.

Each issue of *The Eastside Extra* had three parts. Anika usually wrote the feature story, and Libby was in charge of the photos. The lake would be a great subject for both of them, though Benny still wasn't sure what form his column about helping the community would take. It's not like people could volunteer at a closed-off lake.

"Yes, maybe there'll be some clues around the lake," Anika said. "We should go to the library too, and see if we can learn more about what happened."

CHAPTER TWO

Questions and Investigation

The next day, Benny's mom drove them down the road that passed by the lake. She pulled over to let Benny, Libby, and Anika get a closer look. The friends got out of the car and walked toward the tall fence that stretched all around the lake. Its chain-link sides loomed over them. An official-looking sign attached to it stated:

DO NOT ENTER

THE WATER IS NOT SAFE

SWIMMING AND FISHING

PROHIBITED

Libby pulled out her phone to take a picture of it for their story. She adjusted her angle so the sun wouldn't glare off the metal and focused so that the words would be clear. As she tried to get the perfect shot, she spotted another sign farther down the fence.

"What's with the weird plant sign?"

Benny moved closer and read the words below the leafy logo.

"*EPA Superfund Site.* Huh. I have never seen a sign like this before. I know *EPA* stands for 'Environmental Protection Agency,' but what's a Superfund site?"

Libby moved closer to him. "I don't know, but let's get a picture of that sign too."

Anika followed. "Does it mean we get super funding? Like, a ton of money? Why would anyone waste money on a lake with such bad water?"

Libby had asked Benny to bring his fishing pole so she could take a photo of him by the lake. But now his shadow was blocking the sign. "Can you step back?" she asked. "I need to get this lighting right."

Benny and Anika wandered along the fence while Libby snapped photos. Through the links of the fence, they saw the lake glittering in the sun. It was hard to see what made it unsafe.

"I wonder what that shadow over there is." Anika pointed to where a murky shape clouded the water.

"Gross," Benny said. "Is there something under the water?" The dark shape looked almost like floating dirt, but that didn't make any sense.

Anika gripped the fence and pressed her face up against the links. "No idea. We can't even get close enough to see."

Just then, Benny's mom called, "Are you three all done now? I still have to go to the grocery store before that phone call at three."

"Coming, Mom," Benny said, disappointed. He'd hoped to uncover the lake's secret, but all they'd found was a weird smudge and a mysterious sign with a word he didn't recognize.

Anika noticed his disappointment. "Hey, don't give up yet!" she said as they walked back to Libby and the car. "We just need to do a little more re-search. I'm sure we can find out what *Superfund* means at the library."

Benny's mom agreed to drop them off on her way to the store, so the friends went there next.

West Grove Public Library was their favorite place to go in the summer. Libby had even volun-teered there last year.

Unlike the park, where the friends ended up sweating when the sun was high, the library had air-conditioning and stayed blissfully cool. And Mr. Jefferson, the librarian, always welcomed them— though they had to make sure not to talk too loudly, or he'd shush them with a look that made them want to sink into the ground.

But today, that wouldn't be a problem. They had a question to ask him.

The moment the friends entered the library, Anika made a beeline for the reference desk.

"We have a research project," she began, a little too loudly. Mr. Jefferson gestured for her to keep her voice down.

"Sorry," she whispered. "We have something important to look up, though."

Mr. Jefferson smiled. "What resources have you used so far?"

"Um, a sign?" Benny said. "The fence by the lake says it's an EPA Superfund site. I know the EPA is about the environment, but I don't know anything about Superfunds. Where would we even start to look?"

Mr. Jefferson walked them over to a computer station and pulled up an extra chair. "The first place to start is with what you already know. Your sign mentioned the Environmental Protection Agency, so let's see if they have anything about it on their website. The EPA is a government agency, so it would have an official page. How could we find it?"

"We could do a search for 'EPA,'" Libby said. "And then choose the website ending in '.gov' to make sure it's official."

Mr. Jefferson typed what Libby had suggested and clicked the top result. A blue-and-green government website loaded.

"Hey, there's a search bar." Benny pointed at the screen. "We can look up *Superfund*."

Mr. Jefferson looked over his shoulder. A small line was forming at the reference desk.

"I think you three can take it from here," he said. "Let me know what you find!"

Benny and Anika both dived for the mouse at the same time. It clattered off the desk and onto the floor.

At the sound of the crash, they looked over their shoulders to make sure the librarian hadn't heard anything. Luckily for them, the line in front of Mr. Jefferson's desk had grown, so he just smiled and shook his head.

Libby picked up the mouse off the floor and sat in front of the computer. "Well, that was embarrassing," she said. "I know you two get excited about research, but I think I should handle this today."

She typed *Superfund* into the search bar, clicked on the first link, and grew still and quiet.

Anika peered over Libby's shoulder to read for herself.

"It's a program for cleaning up the most contaminated land in the country," she whispered. "The lake didn't look *that* dirty."

"There was that weird shadow that sort of looked like a spill," Benny pointed out. "I guess we wouldn't want to fish there even if we could."

"But what would the spill be? It's not like we have oil or factories in West Grove." Anika leaned on the back of Libby's chair. She pointed to the bottom of the screen. "What's that map?"

Libby's cursor hovered over their state. "It's

all the Superfund sites—the places where they're cleaning stuff up. Look, there's a diamond right next to West Grove."

"Excuse me!" someone called out behind them. It was an elderly woman they'd seen around the library before.

"Excuse me," the woman repeated, "are you done using the computer?"

"Actually, we're in the middle of something—" Anika began.

Benny knew she was just focused on finding out as much about the lake as they could before his mom picked them up, but he thought she sounded a little rude.

"It's okay," he told the woman. "We were just

looking up some facts about the lake. Should I move this out of the way?" Benny grabbed the chair sitting in front of the desk. The woman was using a wheelchair, and he thought the chair might be blocking her path to the computer.

"Yes, please, that would be very helpful," the woman said. Then she glanced at the computer screen. "I remember when we first found out about that lake."

Benny stopped moving the chair. "When you found out what? That it was a Superfund site?"

"That it was polluted!" The woman jabbed her finger in the air for emphasis. "It's full of coal ash. Ms. Ramirez told us. She spent so much time convincing us all that it wasn't safe, and she was right! But that was many years ago now. You kids wouldn't remember."

Anika knew with every bit of journalistic instinct in her that this was the key to the lake's story. Maybe even the perfect interview for *The Eastside Extra*!

"Does Ms. Ramirez still live here? We'd love to ask her all about the lake."

"Of course. The lake was her passion! I'll give you her phone number."

Anika grinned. Their newsletter would have a feature story after all.

CHAPTER THREE

The Phone Call

As they waited outside the library for Benny's mom to pick them up, the three friends buzzed with excitement. They split up tasks for the next day, which was supposed to be even hotter and stickier than this one.

"I'll do the research and come up with questions to ask." Anika couldn't wait for the interview to get started. Her questions would get right to the bottom of the mystery.

"I could call Ms. Ramirez, but I already promised to spend time with Tío Jorge tonight. He's going back in a week, and it'll be a long time before we get to see him again."

"Don't worry about it. I'll call her," Libby said, immediately regretting that she hadn't volunteered to do the research instead. She hated making phone calls. Libby always felt a little nervous talking to people she didn't know, but she usually had her friends with her to reassure her.

"Thanks, Libby!" Benny flopped on the library's lawn. "Wow, it's hot. Are you sure tomorrow will be worse? My dad says summer here is fine because it was even hotter in Cuba when he was a kid, and I bet Tío Jorge thinks this is nothing compared to Florida."

Anika sprawled on the grass as well. "I mean,

they're not wrong. It's way cooler here than it was back in Mumbai. But just think, before the swimming pool was built a few years ago, people had no place but the lake to cool off all summer. I bet it wasn't easy to close the lake."

"The lady at the library said it was years and years ago that Ms. Ramirez started telling people about it. That coal ash must be really bad if we still can't swim there," Libby said. She winced as she spotted a crushed soda can on the grass. "That should be in the recycling," she muttered. "Speaking of polluting . . ."

Just then, a blue sedan turned the corner. "That's your mom!" Libby called out.

It wasn't just Benny's mom. Tío Jorge had come along for the ride.

"I hear you went to the lake, Benny," his uncle said. "Did you catch anything, or is it still closed?"

Benny's mom laughed. "That lake has been closed for a long time."

Tío Jorge looked at their empty hands. "I see you didn't take any books out. Have you read everything there already?" he joked.

Benny wanted to explain, but he also wanted to surprise Tío Jorge with the story of the lake once they'd put all the pieces together. There was still too much they didn't know.

"We were just doing some research," he said vaguely. "Can we turn on the AC? It's so hot today."

As the air-conditioning cranked up, Tío Jorge said, "That's why it would be great if the lake was open. Just think of all the fun you could have this summer!"

Benny agreed, but he thought that the mystery of the closed lake was enough to keep them busy for a while.

———————————

Back at her house, Libby ignored her brothers, who were still arguing over who had actually hit the baseball into Mr. Grayson's window, and went to her room to make the phone call.

She glanced through the photos she'd taken at the lake to reassure herself before tapping the number into her phone—making phone calls to total strangers was definitely not one of her strengths, but photography definitely was. So was making things beautiful.

Libby also loved working on *The Eastside Extra*

with her friends. She knew this call would be crucial to getting their newsletter its feature story. And by making it, she'd be helping Benny spend time with his uncle.

You can do this, Libby told herself. Then she took a deep breath and tapped the call button.

As the phone rang, Libby thought about what to say. What if she came off as rude? What if Ms. Ramirez didn't pick up at all? Or what if she thought it was a spam call?

"Hello, this is Olivia Ramirez. May I ask who's calling?" The reedy voice on the other end was polite but slightly annoyed.

"Hi, this is . . . this is *The Eastside Extra!*" Libby

thought fast. "We want to interview you about your work on the lake."

There was a long pause.

"I've never heard of *The Eastside Extra*," the voice said. "What is it?"

Libby's stomach started to flutter nervously. "Um, we just started this year."

She didn't want Ms. Ramirez to expect a newspaper with tons of publicity, so she said, "We're an online newsletter. Um, not a very big one. It's just me and two other middle schoolers."

"Oh, is this a school project? It's about time they taught you kids some local history. I'd be happy to meet you for an interview."

"That would be great! Thank you!" Libby said.

Her heart was still beating fast, but she felt more excited than scared. "When would be a good time for you to meet?"

"I'm retired now," Ms. Ramirez said, "so I've got plenty of time. When do you and your friends want to come by?"

"Tomorrow would be good!"

It wasn't exactly a school project, but Libby wanted to seize the opportunity.

The thin voice replied, "My address is 40 Willow Drive. You can come by at 1:30 p.m. tomorrow, after lunch. I'd love to tell you all about what happened to that lake."

Then—*click*—Ms. Ramirez hung up.

Libby pumped her fist and cheered silently.

She'd done it! And once she got started, it hadn't even been that bad.

CHAPTER FOUR

Interviewing Ms. Ramirez

The next day, Libby, Benny, and Anika met on the corner of Willow Drive and Madison Avenue, which was a short walk from Ms. Ramirez's house.

As they'd been warned, the sun was high in the sky and the heat was ferocious. Benny had completely wilted by the time Libby arrived.

"What took you so long?" he moaned.

"More trouble next door," Libby said. "Mr. Grayson is still mad about his window. My parents already said we'd pay to fix it, but now he wants us to replace the shutters too."

"What? Why?" Benny asked.

"I don't know!" Libby said. "My brothers didn't even hit the shutters, let alone break them!"

"Not very neighborly, if you ask me," Anika said.

Libby shook her head in agreement. "And then on the way, we found a traffic sign that was knocked over, so we had to call someone to fix it. Eastside's great, don't get me wrong, but half the time, no one fixes anything or even notices it."

The knocked-over sign had given Libby an idea for her column. But first, they needed to focus on the interview.

"Are you ready to talk with Ms. Ramirez?" she asked.

"Yes, thanks for setting up the interview," Anika said. She pulled up a note on her phone. "I've got seven questions here, in order from the broadest to the most specific. And I did some background research too. Coal ash isn't just one thing," she explained. "There are at least four different types. It's basically anything that's left over when you burn coal. It can be sludgy or glassy or powdery—but you don't want any of it in your water because of the chemicals in it."

"What kind of chemicals?" Libby asked, pulling out her phone to write some of this down.

"I don't remember all of them, but some were mercury and arsenic, which are dangerous."

Benny tried to remember anything he'd heard about those two chemicals. "There's this old black-and-white movie where they poison people with arsenic."

"That doesn't sound good," Libby said.

"Actually, it's really funny—the movie, I mean," he clarified as Libby's jaw dropped. "It was a comedy. Arsenic in the lake isn't funny."

"Glad we agree on that."

Anika looked at the time. "We should hurry up or we'll be late. It's already 1:25 p.m."

She and Libby took off running.

"Can't we just walk?" Benny called after them. "It's too hot to run." But he followed behind, hoping that Ms. Ramirez's house would be cooler than outside.

An overhead fan spun at top speed as they sat down in Ms. Ramirez's living room and picked at slices of kiwi and orange. Ms. Ramirez had brought out a plate of fruit for them to eat, but so far, she hadn't said anything about the lake.

"Eat up, eat up! Have an orange! My grand-kids love them." She sank into a comfortable old armchair.

"Thank you," said Anika, "but if it's okay with you, we'd like to get started with the interview." She pulled out her phone. "Do you mind if we record it? So we can write it down accurately later?"

"Sure, of course you can. I won't say anything to you that I haven't told everyone in West Grove previously. It's the lake you're here about, isn't it? For school."

"Not for school exactly." Benny hoped she wouldn't get mad at them if it wasn't an academic project. He really wanted to hear her story. And he didn't want to have run here on such a hot day for nothing.

Besides, her work sounded exactly like the kind of thing he wanted to write about for *The Eastside Extra*—people trying to make their communities a better place. That gave him a place to start.

"Could you tell us when you realized the lake was unsafe and why you decided to take action?" Benny asked.

Ms. Ramirez sat up straight in the armchair. "At

first, it was hard to prove anything. But I always thought it was a bad idea for them to have an ash pond so near the lake."

"What's an ash pond?" Benny asked, at the same time as Anika said, "Who's *them*?"

Ms. Ramirez answered Anika's question first. "The West Grove Lake Power Station, the coal-fired power plant that provided electricity to this whole area. They shut down a while ago, so you wouldn't remember." Ms. Ramirez peeled an orange as she continued. "When you burn coal to make electricity, it creates something called fly ash. It used to just go into the air, but breathing it in can make people sick—give them asthma and all sorts of things. So it seemed like a good idea when they decided to create an ash pond instead."

Then she turned to Benny. "An ash pond is full of wet fly ash and other kinds of coal ash. The idea is that since it's wet, the ash won't fly off into the atmosphere. Instead, it stays put in the pond." Sighing, she added, "If only it had."

Benny could imagine how happy the residents of West Grove would have been when the air got cleaner. "So what was the problem with this ash pond? It sure sounded like it was a good idea, but we know the lake is all messed up now. You can even see this dark shadow on part of it."

Ms. Ramirez took a long time to chew her orange slice, the silence broken only by the whirring of the ceiling fan. "It did seem like a good idea—which was why no one wanted to hear what I had to say. The ash pond was too close to the lake, and it also wasn't lined properly. Nowadays, people put a special lining around ash ponds so the chemicals won't leak out and get into the surrounding land or water. But back then, they just put a wall around it called an embankment. West Grove is lucky we never used the lake for drinking water, because it was polluted even before that shadow appeared."

"How did you know?" Anika wanted to get all the details. "How could you prove the lake was polluted when it looked normal?"

Ms. Ramirez chuckled. "It's true that I'm not a scientist—I had to teach myself so much as I investigated the ash pond. But I had a good friend working at a lab, and she offered to test the fish I caught and the water itself. The fish were the biggest clue."

Benny thought about people like his uncle sitting by the lake with their fishing rods and bait jars, reeling in a bass or a trout. "Were the fish dying?" he asked.

"No," Ms. Ramirez said. "But they didn't look quite right. They didn't look healthy. And then, when my friend tested them, she found lead and arsenic."

"Anika told us that there's arsenic in coal ash," Libby said. "Also, wow, these kiwis are really good." She had finished almost the entire plate.

"I'm glad you like them." Ms. Ramirez stood up to get some more food from the kitchen. "Excuse me for a minute."

While she sliced more fruit, the three friends stayed in the living room and discussed where to take the interview next. They already had the makings of a great story for their newsletter, but something was missing.

"What I want to know," Anika said, "is where that shadow on the lake comes from. Just chemicals leaking into the lake wouldn't look like that, would they?"

"And we should find out how Ms. Ramirez got people to listen to her," Benny added. "We know the lake's shut down now, but how did that happen?"

"I want to know how the EPA got involved," Libby said, remembering the signs she'd carefully photographed.

"I can tell you all about that." Ms. Ramirez had returned from the kitchen. "But first, you should answer some of my questions. What's this *Eastside Extra* you're interviewing me for, and why do you want to know about the lake? I thought it was a school project, but you said it's not that either."

Libby felt a little bad about not having explained properly. But Ms. Ramirez felt less scary with her sliced kiwis and passion for the environment than she had as a stranger over the phone. She might even find their newsletter interesting.

"We call it *The Eastside Extra*. It's our newsletter about everything going on in Eastside and the rest of West Grove. Except it's been a while since we've sent out an issue, because nothing's been happening this summer. It's been so quiet."

Ms. Ramirez sipped the cup of tea she'd brought back with her from the kitchen when she went to get more food. "There's always a story, even if people aren't talking about it. That's what I learned from the lake. When I got the test results, I realized my instincts had been correct. Those fish were, well, fishy. And whatever was doing that to them couldn't be good for humans either."

"Were people still swimming and fishing?" Anika asked.

Ms. Ramirez nodded. "Not everyone ate fish from the lake, but there were plenty of kids who splashed around in it all summer. I was starting to get worried. But no one else seemed to think there was a problem."

"What about the test results?" Anika asked.

"It would take a lot more work to prove where the contamination was coming from, especially since the power plant company didn't want to run the tests itself. After all, they thought they'd solved their fly ash problem. They didn't want to hear that they'd created a new one."

"So what was your strategy?" Benny asked. He wanted to know all about how the lake had gone from a problem no one wanted to acknowledge to being on a national list of toxic sites.

"I started by talking to neighbors, especially the ones who liked to swim or fish. Maybe they were noticing the same things I was. Some of them agreed that more tests should be run to check that the ash pond was safe. Others thought I was obsessed with ruining the power plant's business. 'First it was fly ash in the air, and they fixed that. Now it's fly ash in the water. When will you be happy?'" She seemed to be imitating the voice of someone specific.

"That sounds just like mean Mr. Grayson," Libby said. "He lives next door."

"You live next door to Arnold Grayson? I haven't heard from him in years." Ms. Ramirez sounded almost nostalgic. "And I wouldn't call him mean, just unhappy. You know, he used to work for the power company. Before the spill."

"What spill?" Anika asked. She checked her phone to make sure it was still recording. They were getting to the meat of the story, and she didn't want to miss anything.

"Just as my friends and I were starting to show up at town council meetings and ask when they'd do something about the ash pond leaking, things got even worse. The wall around the ash pond—the embankment I was talking about earlier—well, it broke."

Libby, Benny, and Anika all gasped.

"How come I never heard about this? My mom

has lived here all her life, and she never mentioned it," Benny said. It wasn't that he thought Ms. Ramirez was making it up. But they needed solid proof to put it in their newsletter.

"I saved some newspaper clippings from the day of the accident," Ms. Ramirez said. "You'll see, it's all there. I can make you copies. Luckily, the spill wasn't as bad as it could have been. It happened in the middle of the day, so the workers caught it quickly before it could turn into a major disaster. But it was a wake-up call. The EPA sent people to help, and the town council was suddenly more interested in our ideas about the ash pond. That's when they closed off the lake."

Anika checked her list of questions. The

conversation had gone in unexpected directions, but one of them still fit. "Is that when the lake became a Superfund site? When the EPA got involved?"

Ms. Ramirez smiled at them. "You three really have done your research! Our lake was one of tens of thousands of places around the country put on the list of Superfund sites. It was even supposed to be cleaned up because it got onto the smaller National Priorities List. But there was one big problem. Who was going to pay for it all?"

"The power plant?" Benny guessed. "If they'd built the ash pond better, none of this would have happened."

Ms. Ramirez's smile was rueful. "We thought

it would go like that. I was sure the cleanup would be the easy part. There's a rule called 'the polluter pays,' and it was very clear who was responsible for the ash pond and its leak. Little did I know that the power plant company was having troubles of its own. It went out of business just three years after the leak, and now we get our electricity from the one in Four Oaks."

"So they never had to clean it up?" Libby couldn't believe it.

"The power company doesn't exist anymore," Ms. Ramirez confirmed. "And the Superfund program doesn't have enough money to clean up every site they want to. They have to focus on the worst ones. Our ash spill wasn't as bad as the big one in

Tennessee in 2008. That one happened at midnight, not in the middle of the day, and it caused a billion dollars of damage. After such a big disaster, they had to change the rules about ash ponds. Our spill could have been a lot worse. But because we were so lucky, there wasn't as much effort or funding to clean the lake."

"And that's why it's still closed off," Benny finished for her. "Just like it's been as long as I can remember." After hearing about the strange-looking fish full of chemicals, Benny definitely didn't want to fish in it. But he felt sad that no one was even trying to clean it. Between the power company closing down and the EPA having so many sites to deal with, it sounded like there would be no progress for a long while.

"Can I see some of the old newspaper articles? And if you have any pictures of the lake before the spill, we'd love to see those too." Libby was already planning how before-and-after photos of the lake could really bring the story to life.

"Of course. I'll go get them." As she stood up, Ms. Ramirez turned to Benny. "I know it's disappointing that the lake won't be clean for a long time yet. But closing it off to swimming and fishing was better than letting people get sick. And that by itself is an improvement over where we started."

She disappeared to look for her newspaper articles.

"Well, we've got our story," said Anika, tapping her phone to stop recording.

"And our photos," Libby added.

Benny nodded. "For my section, I want to get people writing letters to our representative about the lake and how long it's been left polluted. Since the spill was a long time ago, everyone outside West Grove must have forgotten about it by now. But if enough people write in, we could try to get more funding to clean it up. Or she could at least talk to the EPA about it." Benny knew their lake still might not be a top priority, but the letters would be a nudge in the right direction.

"I think we still need one more interview," Libby said thoughtfully. Ever since Ms. Ramirez had mentioned the power plant, she'd been thinking they should interview someone who worked there. They needed to hear all sides of the story. "I can't believe I'm saying this, but we need to talk to Mr. Grayson."

CHAPTER FIVE

Mr. Grayson

Mr. Grayson did not take kindly to a group of kids ringing his doorbell.

"Who's there?" he snarled from behind the closed door.

"It's me, Libby."

"Are you here to fix my shutters?" Mr. Grayson opened the door a little bit. "Those hooligan brothers of yours smashed them. And now you're bringing more young hooligans to my house."

Benny started to edge away from the porch. Libby tried to signal silently that this was just Mr.

Grayson's normal attitude and nothing to be too afraid of. But her friend still looked nervous.

"We just want to talk to you," Libby continued, but Mr. Grayson kept ranting about her brothers.

"Are you sure this is a good idea?" Benny whispered. Libby's neighbor didn't seem like the kind of person who'd give them oranges and kiwis and answer all their questions.

Before Libby could answer, Mr. Grayson went on, "Whatever you're selling, I'm not interested. Now go away before I call your parents." And with that, he slammed the door shut.

Libby sighed. Maybe this interview wasn't worth it after all.

As she and Benny turned around to go, Anika called through the door, "It's about the old power plant! We want to know more about it."

No response.

She shrugged. "That's okay, then. We'll just be going."

The door creaked open.

"Why do you want to know about the power plant? It's been bankrupt for ages." Mr. Grayson sounded suspicious but also intrigued.

Anika knew if she mentioned the ash spill, he might clam up again and tell them to clear out. Since he'd worked at the plant, it might sound like she was blaming him, and he for sure wouldn't like that. "We want to learn about West Grove's past. For our newsletter."

"Oh, so you're the newsletter kids?"

To their surprise, he smiled, his wrinkled face becoming less hostile. "That wasn't a bad article on veterans you wrote. I suppose it's better for children to be writing about our town's history than throwing things at my windows."

Libby bit her tongue. Her brothers hadn't been throwing things at his windows on purpose, just trying to play baseball. But she could keep quiet for as long as it took.

Who knew Mr. Grayson read *The Eastside Extra*? What other secrets was her crabby neighbor hiding?

"We can sit on the porch," Mr. Grayson said, coming outside. "I don't want you kids breaking my wife's china."

They sat down gingerly on the porch's wicker furniture, being careful not to bump or break anything—otherwise, Mr. Grayson's opinions of "hooligan kids" would just be confirmed.

"Now, that power plant," Mr. Grayson began, "gave me my first job when I came back from the Army. It was good work, supplying electricity to the county, and it paid well too. I could be proud of what I was doing."

A creak interrupted him, and he snapped at Anika, "Don't rock in that chair, young lady!"

It was, in fact, a rocking chair, so not rocking was difficult. But Anika did her best to keep it still. She wasn't going to lose their story now.

"I was especially proud to work on the new electrostatic precipitators that let us collect fly ash instead of releasing it into the atmosphere. Do you know how dirty the air around here was before that?" The space between his eyebrows narrowed.

Anika opened her mouth to say something, but Mr. Grayson kept talking. "No, of course not. You couldn't be more than twelve. Well, because of our new system, the rate of asthma attacks in this town went down. We were doing real good, fitting out the plant with new technology."

Anika thought about asking questions, but since Mr. Grayson clearly still had a lot to say, she let him continue without interruption.

"Then that Olivia Ramirez started agitating

about our new ash pond." He grunted. "She said it was too close to the lake and would ruin the fishing. Maybe, but who cares about a few fish when the air is clean again?"

They were definitely getting a different angle on their story now. Benny could see both sides—Mr. Grayson's pride in the new disposal system and Ms. Ramirez's concern that it had replaced one problem with another.

Mr. Grayson paused to cough into his elbow before continuing. "And then everything went wrong." He paused again, this time lost in memories.

Anika was about to ask a question when he continued. "One day, the pond leaked into the lake. The government showed up and tried to take over the cleanup, but a few of my colleagues at the power plant were doing most of the work. I was a little jealous of them at the time. They were working on the big, important issue, and my skills were in a different area. I didn't know how dangerous what they were doing was." He started to choke up. "Three of them fell ill before more than a few years had passed. We didn't realize how toxic the spill was."

There was a long silence as they all thought quietly.

"And then the company shut down?" Benny asked.

Mr. Grayson swallowed hard and continued. "Between those employees suing because they'd been exposed to toxic waste and the EPA demanding the company pay for the cleanup, West Grove Power Station was finished. It went under and took half my pension with it. They were as careful as any other power plant in those days—we know a lot more about coal ash now. But the spill finished them off. Near enough finished me off too. My friends were sick, I didn't have a job, and everybody who knew about the spill gave me dirty looks because I used to say Olivia was on the wrong track about the lake. How was I supposed to know what would happen?"

Anika's rocking chair creaked again, but this time Mr. Grayson had nothing to say.

"I'm sorry," she said, not because of the rocking

noise, but because it sounded like he'd been through hard times.

"Nothing to be sorry for," he said gruffly. "I got another job in industrial engineering. I wasn't exposed to any of the toxic stuff. And everyone's forgotten about it by now. You're not going to dredge it all up in your newsletter, are you?"

Libby didn't see what was wrong with telling everyone what had happened. It had impacted the community in ways that were still obvious today, starting with the Superfund sign on the fence by the lake.

Libby wanted to live in a town where it was safe to swim and where polluters cleaned up their messes. How would they ever get to that world if no one knew how they'd gotten to this one?

But these events had personally impacted her neighbor, and he had been generous enough to share his story with them despite his suspicions. He might be grumpy—and wrong about her brothers and Ms. Ramirez—but he still deserved her consideration. His story mattered.

"We wanted to hear your side of what happened so we could share that too. You and your colleagues also deserve to have your story told. Thank you for letting us hear it. Can we include what you told us in our newsletter?"

They waited in suspense as Mr. Grayson considered it.

"Fine," he huffed. "But, Libby, remind your parents that they still owe me for my damaged shutters."

CHAPTER SIX

Finishing Touches

The next two days were a flurry of typing and formatting. Benny put together an example letter for people who wanted to write to their representative about the lake, and Libby urged readers to send in photographs of things they saw in their community that could use fixing or cleaning up.

"The first step toward fixing things is noticing them," she explained to her friends. She included the knocked-over traffic sign as an example.

Just when the newsletter was almost finished,

a link would break, or a photo would inexplicably double in size, and they'd have to call Benny's dad over to help fix the website he'd helped them create.

Benny couldn't wait to share their newsletter with everyone. But most of all, he wanted Tío Jorge to read it. After all, without his gift of the fishing pole, they wouldn't have had a story.

When Benny asked Tío Jorge to subscribe, he was happy to add to their audience.

"I've hardly had a chance to hang out with you, though," Benny's uncle complained as he confirmed his subscription. "Not that I don't want you to enjoy your summer vacation with your friends, but what about some time for your uncle who's leaving next week? How about I take you and Isabel to the mov-

ies this afternoon?"

Benny really wanted to go, but the newsletter wasn't finished.

"Don't worry," Anika reassured him. "Libby and I can finish the formatting."

Libby nodded. "Go to the movies—it sounds like fun."

Now that he knew he wasn't leaving them in the lurch, Benny felt free to show his excitement. "Can we get popcorn at the theater? And some chocolate-covered gummy bears?"

"They have chocolate-covered gummy bears?" Tío Jorge pretended to be shocked. "I've got to try those—and maybe I'll even let you have a few."

Isabel shrieked with excitement from the next room over. "Chocolate-covered gummy bears?"

"Stop eavesdropping," Benny called, but his sister was already running over and jumping up to hug Tío Jorge.

———————————

By the time they got back from the theater, Benny was feeling worried. He hadn't gotten any texts from Anika or Libby, and finishing the newsletter shouldn't have taken this long. What if something had gone wrong when he wasn't there? What if the computer had crashed and all their work was lost?

You're being silly, he told himself. Libby was probably just adjusting one of the photos for the fiftieth time so it would be perfect.

Tío Jorge locked the car door just as his phone dinged with a new notification.

"Benny, look what's arrived!" Tío Jorge held up his phone. There was *The Eastside Extra*, freshly released and ready to read.

"They did send it out after all!" Benny cheered. "You have to read it, Tío Jorge. You gave us the main story."

He looked uncomfortable. "I'm not sure all of West Grove wants to read about my visit . . ."

"No, not your visit. It's about why we can't go fishing. There's this whole history about the lake and why it's closed off, and you wouldn't believe how much work we did to find it." Benny waved excitedly, almost knocking Tío Jorge's phone out of his hand.

"The reason we can't go fishing," his uncle joked,

"is because you need to learn not to wave things around like that. Imagine the damage you could do with a fishing pole."

Then he ruffled Benny's hair. "But I'm going to read all about your lake. I can't believe you pulled this all together since I arrived in town. It's been less than a week."

Benny smiled. "It wasn't just me. I had a lot of help from Libby and Anika."

While they were talking, Isabel had run up the garage steps and was twisting the handle of the door to the house. She called back to them. "Tío Jorge, can you please stop looking at Benny's newsletter and give me the keys?"

Tío Jorge pulled the keys out of his pocket. "Here

they are, Isabel." Then he turned back to Benny. "I'm really proud of you. And I can't wait to find out everything you've discovered. After all, fishing isn't really about catching fish."

"What do you mean?" Benny asked, confused. Weren't the fish the whole point of fishing? Why else would you spend so much time just sitting outside, especially in the summer when it was so hot?

"It's about spending some quality time with your friends, doing something you all love. And even though my present didn't get used the way I anticipated, you still got to do that. So," Tío Jorge concluded, "I think it was a success."

Benny grinned. "Definitely."

What fishing was to Tío Jorge, the newsletter was to him and Libby and Anika. Benny followed Tío Jorge and Isabel inside to where their family and friends were waiting, ready to celebrate the release of *The Eastside Extra*.

Think About It

1. Libby was nervous about talking to Ms. Ramirez to set up the interview, but she made the call to help her friends. Have you ever done something difficult to help a friend? If so, what was it?

2. The friends interviewed both Ms. Ramirez and Mr. Grayson. Why is it important to hear multiple people's stories when learning about the past?

3. Benny encourages people to write letters to their representative and ask her to help get their lake cleaned. What is one issue in your community that you'd like to see changed? How could you tell your representative about it?

About the Author

Maya Chhabra is the author of a middle grade historical novel, *Stranger on the Home Front*, and a YA verse novel, *Chiara in the Dark*. Her short stories, poetry, and translations have been published in a variety of venues. Follow her writing updates on Twitter at @MChhabraAuthor. Maya lives in Brooklyn with her wife.

About the Illustrator

Nathalie Ortega illustrates children's books from all around the world. Her works are published in countries such as the USA, UK, Australia, Spain, and many others. Companies such as Pearson Education, Longman, Oxford University Press, and HarperCollins have her art in picture books, English Language Teaching materials, schoolbooks, and more. Nathalie loves working at her home studio with her family and three funny kitties.

Explore Other Questions in
The
Eastside Extra

The Eastside Extra

HOW DID WE GET HERE?

Exploring the Ancestry of Eastside Residents

Written by Anita Storey · Illustrated by Nathalie Ortega

The Eastside Extra

PUBLIC FUNDING, PUBLIC DECISIONS

How Eastside Schools Spend Their Money

Written by Anita Storey · Illustrated by Nathalie Ortega

The Eastside Extra

STILL SERVING

The Inside Scoop on One Veteran's Life

Written by Anita Storey · Illustrated by Nathalie Ortega